Anna Grossnickle Hines

Gramma's Walk

 Greenwillow Books, New York

Watercolor paints and colored pencils were used for the full-color art.
The text type is ITC Clearface.

Printed in Hong Kong by South China Printing Company (1988) Ltd.
First Edition   10 9 8 7 6 5 4 3 2 1

Library of Congress Cataloging-in-Publication Data

Hines, Anna Grossnickle.
Gramma's walk / by Anna Grossnickle Hines.
p. cm.
Summary: Donnie and Gramma, who is in a wheelchair, take an
imagined walk to the seashore and smell the salty breeze, walk
barefoot on the warm sand, observe animals, and build a sand castle.
ISBN 0-688-11480-6 (trade).   ISBN 0-688-11481-4 (lib. bdg.)
[1. Grandmothers—Fiction.   2. Seashore—Fiction.
3. Imagination—Fiction.   4. Walking—Fiction.
5. Physically handicapped— Fiction.]   I. Title.
PZ7.H572Gs 1993
[E]—dc20   92-30085   CIP   AC

FOR EVERYONE WHO KNOWS
THAT WITH IMAGINATION
ANYTHING IS POSSIBLE

Donnie slips quietly into the sunroom where Gramma waits.

"There's my boy," she says. "Where shall we walk today?"

Donnie thinks hard. Where does he want to go? The woods, maybe, with the thimbleberries and splotches of sunlight on the path? No, not today.

"The seashore," he says. As he pulls the hassock up close, he's careful not to bump Gramma's wheelchair. "Start by the lighthouse, in the grassy place."

"Ready?" asks Gramma.

Donnie closes his eyes and lays his head on her lap.

"*Shhhklooshhhh.*" Gramma's voice is soft, as if the waves are still a distance away. "*Shhhklooshhhh.*"

Donnie listens and makes a picture in his head of the lighthouse out on the point. He sees the path through the tall grass and thinks about his feet crunching into the dry sand as he walks beside Gramma.

"*Shhhhklooshhhh.* Feel the salty breeze, Donnie? Can you smell it?" Gramma breathes deeply.

Donnie does, too, and feels the cool air filling up his chest.

"Look," Gramma whispers. "There's a rabbit. See it?"

Donnie holds his breath, then lets it out. "I see it, Gramma, and it sees me. I'm holding still so it won't be scared."

Donnie sees the rabbit hop into the tall grass. "Ooops! There it goes."

"Look at the tracks this morning, Donnie. A deer has been here."

Donnie pictures the pointy hoofprints, then sees other prints. Boot prints. Left foot, right foot, and a poked place in the sand. Left foot, right foot, poke. Left foot, right foot, poke. "Somebody went by with a walking stick," he says.

"*Shhhkloooshhhh.*" The waves are closer now. Donnie sees them lapping the sand. "*Shhhklooshhhh.*"

"I'm taking my shoes off, Gramma," he says.

"Good idea!" she says. "I'll take mine off, too. Oh, the dry sand feels warm on my feet."

"I'm by the water," Donnie tells her. "It feels wet and scrunchy here. *Shhhklooshh!* Oooh! The water's cold!"

"Screeaw! Screeaw!"
Gramma calls.
"Seagulls!" says Donnie.
"See them all walking around
with their bumpy knees and
floppy feet?"
Gramma laughs, then calls,
"Whawp-whawp-whawp!"
Donnie sees the seagulls
fly away as he and Gramma
get close.

"Shall we build a castle here?" Gramma asks.

"Yes," Donnie says. "I'll do the tower. You make the walls. I'll get some good wet sand, Gram. Plop! Plop! See how big my tower's getting?"

"I've found a flag for your tower, Donnie. It's a twig with one dry leaf. Do you want to put it in, or shall I?"

"Let me," Donnie says. "There. All done."

"Oh, oh! Here comes the ferry! *Hmmmmmmmm. Hmmmmm.*" He makes the sound as the big white boat glides by.

"*ShhhhhKLOOOPSHHHhhh! ShhhKLOOPSHHHhhh!*" Gramma's waves get bigger from the ferry's wake. "*SHHHHKLOOPSHHHH!*"

"There goes your wall, Gramma. There goes my tower. Just a bump now, but the flag is still there."

"A bump with a flag," Gramma agrees.

"Donga-donga," says Gramma. *"Donga-donga."* It's the song of the buoy out in the water. *"Donga-donga."*

Donnie knows that means they are coming to the rocks. "I'm hopping on the smooth rocks, Gramma." They feel solid under his feet after the scrunchy sand.

"Here come the barnacle rocks," Gramma warns.

"Ouch!" Donnie cries. "Wait till I put my shoes back on."

"Peeeep! Peeeep!"

"Peeper birds," Donnie says. "Where are they, Gramma?"

"Standing on the rocks out in the water," she says. "See their little stick legs and long orange bills?"

"Will we see the otter today, Gramma? Is he on his rock?"

"I don't know, Donnie. What do *you* see?"

"He's there. He's scratching his chin on the barnacles."

"Ummm," says Gramma. "Now he's watching us watch him."

Donnie laughs. "I like the otter, Gramma."

"Me, too. Look, I found a purple jelly bean rock today."

"I found a shell. It curls all around inside. See it, Gramma?"

"I see, Donnie. Are you ready to walk back now?"

"I'm ready, Gramma."

So they go back.

"Here's the otter," Donnie says. "Good-bye, otter."

"Good-bye, peeper birds," says Gramma.

"Good-bye, barnacle rocks," they say. "Good-bye, smooth rocks."

"Our castle flag is still there," Donnie says. "Good-bye, castle flag. Good-bye, lighthouse."

"Good-bye, seashore," Gramma says.

Donnie sighs.

"You know what, Gramma?" he says as he helps push her chair to the table for lunch. "You're the best walker in the whole world."

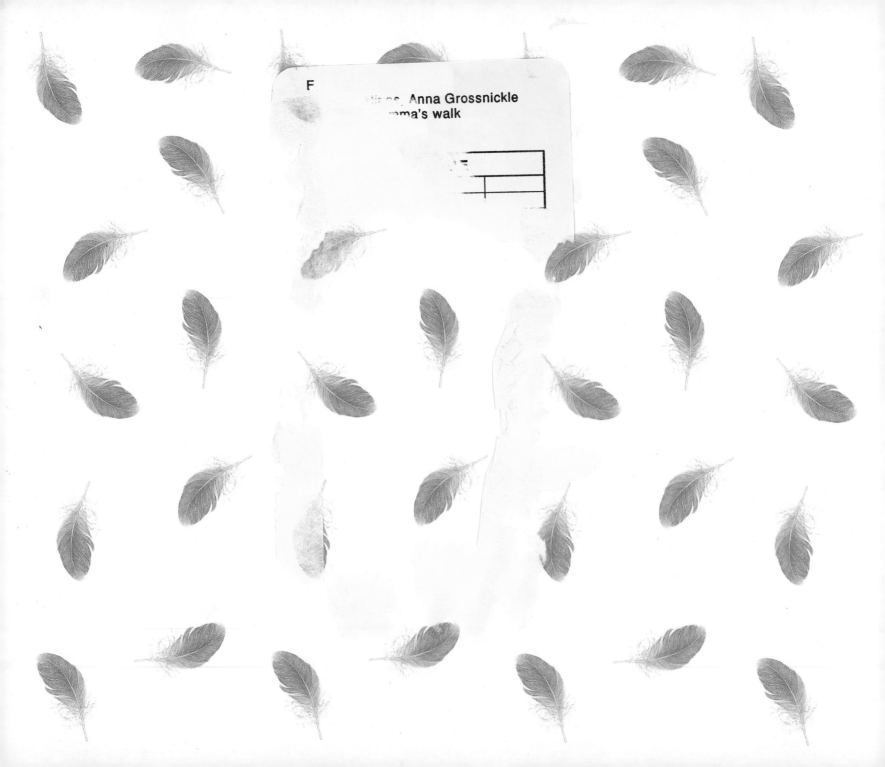